What's So Wonderful About Webster?

B&H
KIDS
Nashville, Tennessee

Dedication

Dedicated to Grant, Cohen, Karis, John, Mia, and Grace. You are fearfully and wonderfully made by God, who loves you more than you know.

ISBN: 978-1-5359-4986-6

Dewey Decimal Classification: C155.2

Subject Heading: SELF-PERCEPTION / SPORTS / SPORTS TOURNAMENTS

Scripture quotations are taken from the The Holy Bible, English Standard Version. Copyright © 2001 by Crossway Bibles, a publishing ministry of Good News Publishers.

Printed in September 2019 in Shenzhen, Guangdong, China.

1 2 3 4 5 6 • 23 22 21 20 19

$\mathcal{A}$ttention everyone!" announced Ms. Pumpernickle. "Friday is field day! I hope everyone in our fourth-grade class will participate. The winning class gets an ice cream party!"

"Yay!" cheered the kids.

"Oh no!" Catherine said. "We will never beat the fifth graders! They are really big."

"But I can run as fast as a bolt of lightning," said Caleb.

"I can jump rope a million times without stopping," bragged Hannah.

Maxwell's hand shot up. "I just got a Frisbee and can do the Frisbee throw."

Emma bounced in her seat. "I can stand on my head for ten minutes without falling over."

"Hey, Webster," whispered Herbert.

"What should I do for field day?"

"You did well at the egg race last year," answered Webster.

"Oh, yeah. Great idea. What are you going to do?"

"Ummm, I can't tell you. . . . It's a surprise," Webster mumbled.

Webster's hands started to sweat. He couldn't think of anything he was good at, except for maybe eating peanut butter, but he was pretty sure that wasn't an event.

The next day at recess, Webster watched Maxwell
throw his new Frisbee. It landed in a tree.

"Aren't you left-handed? Maybe you should throw
with your other hand," Webster suggested.

"Great idea!" Maxwell said.

Webster walked to the corner of the playground to try his new jump rope. After four jumps, he tripped and fell into a bush. Hannah giggled.

"Maybe *you* should jump instead," Webster said.

Hannah untangled the rope and began to jump really fast. But she did not jump a million times, he noticed, only 67.

"You can borrow it if you want to practice," said Webster.

"Really? Thanks!" said Hannah as she ran off.

After school, Webster asked his mom for some eggs and tried carrying them across his yard on a spoon. But he kept dropping them, and soon his yard looked like it had been bombed by an army of chickens.

The next day, Webster tried throwing his Frisbee. But his neighbor's dog, Barfy, caught it and ran off down the street. Webster always thought Barfy was the worst name for a dog.

That night, Webster
tried standing on his head.

His face turned red,
and he felt dizzy.

Then he knocked over a chair and scared the cat.

By Thursday, Webster had tried and failed at every event on the list. *Field day was going to be the worst day of his life.*

At dinner, Webster told his parents the tragic news about field day. He asked if he could stay home the next day because he wasn't feeling well, but Mom said he didn't have a fever.

"Why don't we ask God to help you find what you're good at?" she said.

"But I'm not good at anything," Webster muttered.

"Not true," said his dad. "You're good at lots of things."

Webster wasn't so sure. He could only think of one thing he was good at. He walked to the kitchen to find some peanut butter. The jar was empty. He dropped his head and slowly shuffled back to his room.

At bedtime, Mom and Dad prayed for Webster and gave him a big hug. After they left, he remembered a story in the Bible and got down on his knees to pray.

"Please, God, will you make it rain for forty days and nights and flood the whole earth so field day will be cancelled tomorrow? Amen."

Webster woke up early and looked out the window. The sun was shining brightly. Then he remembered God had promised Noah that He would never flood the earth again. Webster sighed.

At breakfast, his dad read Psalm 139:14. "I praise you, for I am fearfully and wonderfully made. Wonderful are your works; my soul knows it very well."

"Well, *I'm* not wonderful," Webster said.

"You know," his dad said, "the Bible always tells the truth. It says God is good and never makes mistakes. He makes wonderful things. And He had a really good idea when He made you, Webster."

"So you *are* wonderful," said his mom, "even if you don't see it sometimes."

Webster didn't feel wonderful. He felt like a big loser.
*Maybe it will snow in the next hour and
school will be cancelled,* he thought.

Or a giant earthquake . . .

The playground was decorated with banners and balloons. When field day started, everyone cheered, except for Webster. He handed out water and wished he was invisible.

"Hey, Webster!" shouted Herbert. "Have you done an event yet?"

"Uh, not yet," he answered. "I've been really busy with, you know, water."

Principal Diaz blew his whistle. "Gather 'round everyone! These three classes have made it to the final round!"

He held up a sign that said:

- Mr. Dunbar's 5th-grade class: 75 points
- Mrs. Hall's 3rd-grade class: 71 points
- Ms. Pumpernickle's 4th-grade class: 68 points

"Oh, no! The fifth graders are winning," whispered Hannah.

"Each class will choose four runners for the final egg relay," said Principal Diaz. "The winning team will gain eight more points for your class."

Ms. Pumpernickle said, "Webster, you helped give out water all day. I'm going to let you lead the egg relay and choose our final team."

Everyone stared at Webster. His heart was pounding, and his hands were sweating.

"Umm, Caleb, Mia, and Peter run the fastest, so I choose them."

"Great choices!" said Ms. Pumpernickle.

"But I think Herbert should have my spot," Webster said.

"What?" said Ms. Pumpernickle. "Why?"

"Herbert is better than me and didn't drop any eggs last year." Webster handed Herbert his spoon.

When the whistle blew, everyone cheered. Soon the whole field was covered with broken eggs. Everyone had dropped at least one . . . except for Herbert.

Principal Diaz stood up to announce the results. "For the most eggs carried, Ms. Pumpernickle's class gets eight more points for a total of 75 points. They are now tied for first place with Mr. Dunbar's fifth-grade class. As a tiebreaker, we will have a tug-of-war to see who will win field day."

Everyone in Webster's class sighed. They knew they would never beat the fifth graders in a tug-of-war.

Everyone that is . . . except for Webster, who raised his hand.

"Yes, Webster?" asked Principal Diaz.

Webster cleared his throat and said, "Sixty-eight plus eight is 76."

Principal Diaz stared at Webster with a confused look and then looked back at the scoreboard.

"Oh my. I'm so sorry! You're right, Webster. Ms. Pumpernickle's class actually has 76 points. *That means they win field day!*"

Mr. Dunbar's
5th-grade class:
75 points

Mrs. Hall's
3rd-grade class:
71 points

Ms. Pumpernickle's
4th-grade class:
75 points

Webster's class went wild with cheers. After the medal ceremony, they hurried to their room for ice cream.

"Class, I'm so proud of you!" announced Ms. Pumpernickle. "I want to especially thank Webster."

"But I didn't score any points or do anything," he muttered.

"Not true," she continued. "You picked the winning relay team, you gave your slot to Herbert, and you had the math skills and courage to tell Principal Diaz our class had won."

Maxwell raised his cone. "Webster helped me with my Frisbee. I used my left hand and got first place."

"He let me use his jump rope, and I got third place," said Hannah.

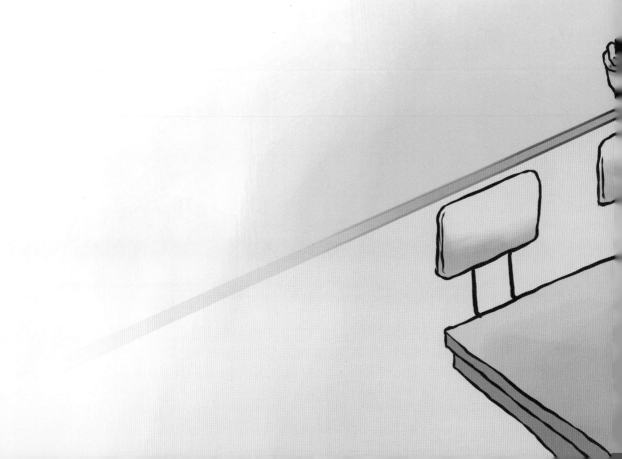

"Class," said Ms. Pumpernickle, "raise your hand if you got hot today and Webster gave you water."

Almost everyone raised their hands.

"Webster, you may be the most important person on our team. We would not have won field day if it hadn't been for you."

Webster couldn't believe his ears. He ended up smiling the rest of the day.

At dinner, he told his parents all about field day.

"Webster, I'm so proud," his mom said. "We prayed for God to show you what you were good at, and He answered that prayer."

"That's right, son," his dad said. "You are a leader. Jesus said that good leaders help others, and you helped your whole class today. I wouldn't be surprised if one day you become a principal or pastor or maybe the president."

Webster's eyes widened as he listened to his parents' encouragement.

That night, Webster stared at his medal. He looked up and whispered, "Thank You, God, for not flooding the whole earth today. And thanks for Mom and Dad and my friends and teacher. And thanks for helping me be good at math and at being a leader. And thanks for making me. I'm glad You did. You must be a good leader too, God. The best ever. And when I grow up, I want to be just like You."

Remember:

I praise you, for I am fearfully and wonderfully made. Wonderful are your works; my soul knows it very well. —*Psalm 139:14* ESV

Read:

Read Psalm 139:13–15 in your Bible. These verses say that God knew us before we were even born. He "knit" us together. Knitting is a detailed process that takes skill and attention. So these verses are explaining that the work of forming each and every human was a careful and intricate process. This kind of special creation points to something bigger—God the creator!

   At times we may each wonder what makes us so wonderful. We may doubt there is anything remarkable about us at all. But because God took such special care in each and every part of our creation, we can know we were not simply thrown together. We were created with a special and specific purpose. Don't let what makes you unique seem unimportant. After all, you were wonderfully made!

Think:

1. Webster didn't think God had made him wonderful. Have you ever felt the same way? When?

2. Make a list of qualities that make your friends and family special. Share the list with each of them!

3. Think about how carefully God made each of us. None of us is exactly the same! Can you list three things that are unique about you?

4. Ask your friends and family what they think makes you wonderful. Were you surprised at their answers?

5. Webster realized that being willing and able to help people was something that made him wonderful. What about you? Can you think of a new wonderful quality God gave you?